Bob the Builder™

A Surprise for Wendy

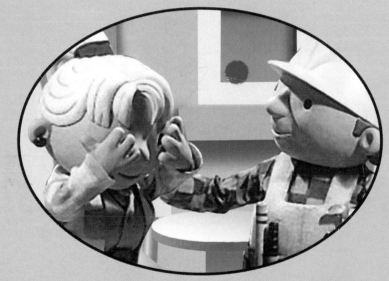

by Alison Inches
illustrated by Diane Dubreuil

Ready-to-Read

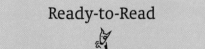

Simon Spotlight

New York   London   Toronto   Sydney   Singapore

Based upon the television series *Bob the Builder*™
created by HIT Entertainment PLC and Keith Chapman,
with thanks to HOT Animation, as seen on Nick Jr.®

SIMON SPOTLIGHT
An imprint of Simon & Schuster Children's Publishing Division
1230 Avenue of the Americas, New York, New York 10020
Manufactured in the United States of America
First Edition
2 4 6 8 10 9 7 5 3 1

Library of Congress Cataloging-in-Publication Data

Inches, Alison.
A surprise for Wendy / by Alison Inches ;—1st ed.
p. cm—(Bob the builder. Preschool ready-to-read ; 4)
Summary: While Wendy is gone for the day, Bob the builder and the others
fix up her garden to surprise her.
ISBN 0-689-84754-8
[1. Surprise—Fiction. 2. Friendship—Fiction. 3. Gardens—Fiction.
4. Trucks—Fiction] I. Titles. II. Series.

Pz7.S96563 2002
[E]—dc21   2001049797

"I am late!" said .
WENDY

"And my  is a mess!"
GARDEN

"Your  can wait,"
GARDEN

said . "You have a
BOB

train to catch."

 picked up 's .

SCOOP   WENDY   SUITCASE

"Good-bye!" said .

WENDY

"Good-bye!"
said  and .
BOB   DIZZY
"**Meow!**" said .
PILCHARD

"What will we do without  ?" asked .

WENDY

DIZZY

"I know! We can surprise  and clean

WENDY

up her ," said.

GARDEN   BOB

"This will be fun!"
said .

DIZZY

"Rock and Roll!"
said .

ROLEY

"We have to work fast," said . " will be home by ."

BOB   WENDY

SIX O'CLOCK

The machines
got to work.

mixed the 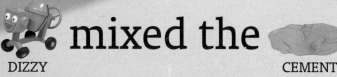.

DIZZY   CEMENT

Slosh! Slosh!

 flattened the .

ROLEY   DIRT

Rumble! Rumble!

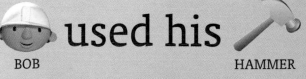 used his 🔨.

BOB   HAMMER

Bang! Bang!

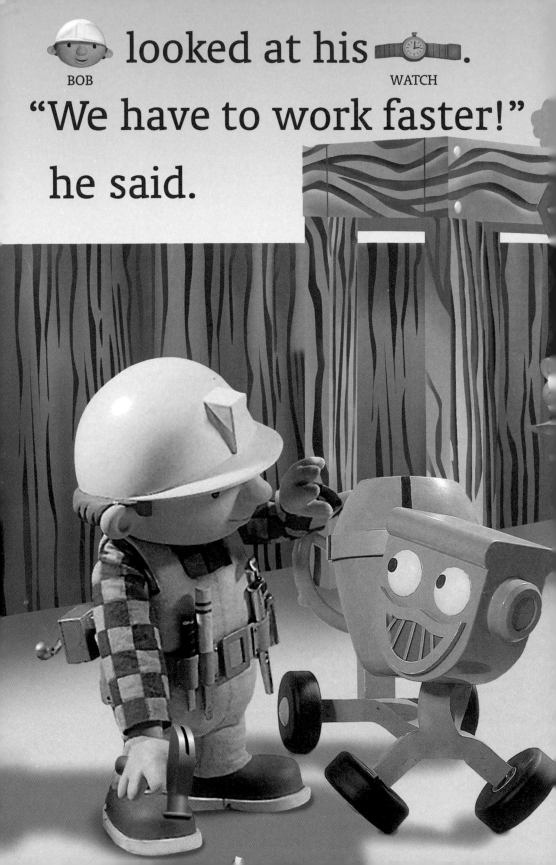

 looked at his .

BOB

WATCH

"We have to work faster!"

he said.

So the machines
worked faster.

**Slosh! Slosh!
Rumble! Rumble!
Bang! Bang!**

spread the .

DIZZY   CEMENT

 scooped the 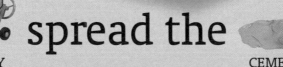.

MUCK   DIRT

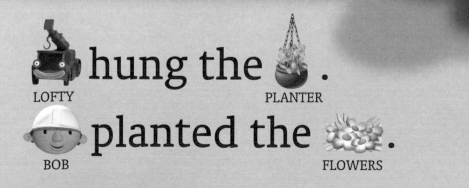

LOFTY hung the PLANTER.

BOB planted the FLOWERS.

Slosh! Slosh!

Rumble! Rumble!

Bang! Bang!

"Hello!" said.
WENDY
"I am home!" Then
she put down her 🧳.
SUITCASE

"I am HOME!" shouted  WENDY.
The machines stopped
working.

"Surprise!" said 🪖.
BOB

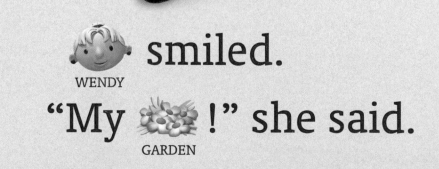 smiled.

WENDY

"My 🌸 !" she said.

GARDEN

"Did we fix it?"

asked .

SCOOP

"Yes, you did!" said .

WENDY

"My new  is perfect,"
GARDEN
said .
WENDY
"Hooray!" said .
BOB
"Thank you!" said .
WENDY